Max's Christmas
ROSEMARY WELLS

A TRUMPET CLUB SPECIAL EDITION

For Beezoo Wells

Published by The Trumpet Club
666 Fifth Avenue, New York, New York 10103

Copyright © 1986 by Rosemary Wells

ISBN 0-440-84358-8

This edition published by arrangement with Dial Books for
Young Readers, a division of Penguin Books USA Inc.

Designed by Atha Tehon

The full-color artwork consists of black line-drawings
and full-color washes. The black line is prepared and
photographed separately for greater sharpness and contrast.
The full-color washes are prepared with colored inks. They
are then camera-separated and reproduced as red,
yellow, blue, and black halftones.

Printed in the United States of America
November 1991

10 9 8 7 6 5 4 3
UPC

Guess what, Max!
said Max's sister Ruby.
What? said Max.

It's Christmas Eve, Max, said Ruby,
and you know who's coming!
Who? said Max.

Santa Claus is coming,
that's who, said Ruby.
When? said Max.

Tonight, Max, he's coming tonight!
said Ruby.
Where? said Max.
Spit, Max, said Ruby.

Santa Claus is coming right down
our chimney into our living room,
said Ruby.
How? said Max.

That's enough questions, Max.

You have to go to sleep fast,
before Santa Claus comes, said Ruby.

But Max wanted to stay up
to see Santa Claus.
No, Max, said Ruby.

Nobody ever sees Santa Claus.
Why? said Max.
BECAUSE! said Ruby.

But Max didn't believe a word
Ruby said.

So he sneaked downstairs...

and waited for Santa Claus.

Max waited a long time.

Suddenly, ZOOM! Santa
jumped down the chimney
into the living room.

Don't look, Max! said Santa Claus.
Why? said Max.
Because, said Santa Claus,
nobody is supposed to see me!

Why? said Max.
Because everyone is supposed to be
asleep in bed, said Santa Claus.

But Max peeked at Santa anyway.
Guess what, Max! said Santa Claus.
What? said Max.

It's time for me to go away
and you to go to sleep,
said Santa Claus.
Why? said Max.

BECAUSE! said Santa Claus.

Ruby came downstairs.
What happened, Max? asked Ruby.
Who were you talking to?
Where did you get that hat?

Max! Why is your blanket
so humpy and bulgy?

BECAUSE! said Max.